HERGÉ
★
THE ADVENTURES OF
TINTIN
★
THE SHOOTING STAR

EGMONT

The TINTIN books are published in the following languages:

Alsacien	CASTERMAN
Basque	ELKAR
Bengali	ANANDA
Bernese	EMMENTALER DRUCK
Breton	AN HERE
Catalan	CASTERMAN
Chinese	CASTERMAN/CHINA CHILDREN PUBLISHING
Corsican	CASTERMAN
Danish	CARLSEN
Dutch	CASTERMAN
English	EGMONT UK LTD/LITTLE, BROWN & CO.
Esperanto	ESPERANTIX/CASTERMAN
Finnish	OTAVA
French	CASTERMAN
Gallo	RUE DES SCRIBES
Gaumais	CASTERMAN
German	CARLSEN
Greek	CASTERMAN
Hebrew	MIZRAHI
Indonesian	INDIRA
Italian	CASTERMAN
Japanese	FUKUINKAN
Korean	CASTERMAN/SOL
Latin	ELI/CASTERMAN
Luxembourgeois	IMPRIMERIE SAINT-PAUL
Norwegian	EGMONT
Picard	CASTERMAN
Polish	CASTERMAN/MOTOPOL
Portuguese	CASTERMAN
Provençal	CASTERMAN
Romanche	LIGIA ROMONTSCHA
Russian	CASTERMAN
Serbo-Croatian	DECJE NOVINE
Spanish	CASTERMAN
Swedish	CARLSEN
Thai	CASTERMAN
Tibetan	CASTERMAN
Turkish	YAPI KREDI YAYINLARI

TRANSLATED BY
LESLIE LONSDALE-COOPER AND MICHAEL TURNER

EGMONT
We bring stories to life

Artwork copyright © 1946 by Editions Casterman, Paris and Tournai.
Copyright © renewed 1974 by Casterman.
Text copyright © 1978 by Egmont UK Limited.
First published in Great Britain in 1961 by Methuen Children's Books.
This edition published in 2002 by Egmont UK Limited,
239 Kensington High Street, London W8 6SA.

Library of Congress Catalogue Card Numbers Afor 5878 and R 585355
ISBN 978 1 4052 0621 1

Printed in China
7 9 10 8

THE SHOOTING STAR

Very odd! Why did they ring off so abruptly? . . . Crumbs, how hot it is! Phew! . . .

?

I can't believe my eyes! It's getting bigger every minute!

All very peculiar . . . and I'm going to get to the bottom of it. Come on, Snowy . . . to the Observatory.

RRRRING

OBSERVATORY

Definitely, it's bigger than ever! . . .

I'd like to have a word with the Director, please.

Impossible. The Director is engaged.

?

SLAM

OBSERVATORY

That's the limit! Slamming the door in my face!

What a nerve!

RRRING RRING

You again? . . . I told you before, the Director's engaged. He can't . . .

That doesn't matter now . . . The Observatory's on fire! . . .

Good gracious! Where?

Here, come and look . . .

?!

SLAM

How strangely quiet and empty it all is . . . as if there weren't a soul . . .

Ah, there's somebody.

A judgement! Woe!

Excuse me, sir, could you tell me . . .

That's what I told them: "It's a judgement."

A judgement! Yea! . . . A judgement, and don't you forget it!

NO ENTRY

NO ENTRY

RAT RAT TAT

RAT TAT

TAT TAT TAT

NO ENTR

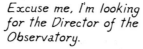

Excuse me, I'm looking for the Director of the Observatory.

Ssh! It's me!

It's me, but ssh! . . . Silence! Don't disturb my colleague; he's deep in some very complicated mathematics. While he's finishing, have a look through the telescope, if you like; it's a sight worth seeing.

Let's have a look.

OH!

?

Good heavens, sir! It's horrible . . . horrible!

Yes, in one sense it's horrible . . .

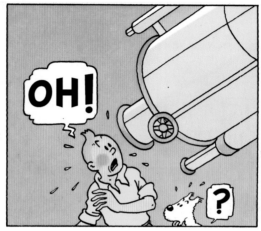

It's enormous! Simply enormous!

Enormous, yes!

And its hairy legs! . . . It makes me shiver to think of them!

Its legs? . . . What legs?

What legs? . . . Why, belonging to that gigantic spider . . .

Spider? . . . Is this your idea of a joke young man?

Come and see for yourself!

By the rings of Saturn! . . . You're right . . . It is, quite definitely, a spider! . . .

You see now!

How extraordinary! Extraordinary! . . . It has characteristics of Meta segmentata . . . At least . . . No! It's an Araneus diadematus! An enormous Araneus diadematus!

Anyway, it's a spider! Ugh! What a monster! . . . And it's travelling through space . . . Supposing it . . . ??

Hello, Professor . . . I've found the answer . . . It was a spider walking across the lens! . . . It's gone now . . .

A spider? . . . A harmless little spider! That's all it was, scaring them out of their wits! . . . This'll kill me!

WOOAH!

Come and look now . . .

Well?

It looks like . . . It looks like a huge ball of fire . . .

It IS a ball of fire! . . . A VA-A-A-A-AST ball of fire . . .

?

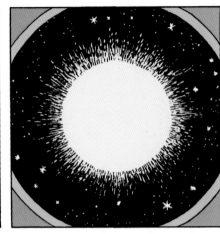

Yes, it's a gigantic mass of matter in fusion . . .

But why is it growing bigger . . . before our very eyes? . . . Because it is growing, isn't it?

Naturally it's growing bigger – it's heading towards us, at an incredible speed.

Heading towards us? . . . But if it keeps on coming . . . ?

Yes! . . . That fire-ball is going to collide with the Earth!

Great heavens! But that'll mean . . .

. . . THE END OF THE WORLD, YES!

Look here Mr Prophet, why don't you go home? You'd be better off in bed! . . .

You hear that? He dares to set himself up against Philippulus the prophet . . . An advocate of the devil! . . . A son of Satan! . . . A tool of Beelzebub!

Get back to Satan, your Master!

Oyez, there will be a plague! Bubonic plague! . . . and fever! The end of the world is upon us, servant of Satan!

That fellow gets on my nerves!

Here we are, home at last!

What a blinding light!

OWW!

?

Crumbs! The window frame is so hot I burnt myself! . . .

Poor old Snowy . . . dying for a drink. And that poor little plant's all wilted.

The end of the world, Snowy! . . . The END of the world! . . . The end of the WORLD! D'you understand, Snowy?

DONG DONG

Return to your Master, the Prince of Darkness!

There! . . . Now I hope he'll leave me in peace!

I think I'll have a bit of a rest. I'm absolutely worn out . . .

Phew! . . . I've had enough of this.

DONG

How did you get in here?

Prophets come and go as they please!

I don't know how you got in, but I know jolly well how you're going out! And get a move on!

Using threats now, eh?

You sit down! And take a look at what I've brought you.

Yes! Behold the judgement! An enormous spider!

ARANEUS DIADEMATUS

LIFE-SIZE

DONG DONG DONG

Get out! Leave me alone!

DONG DONG

Great snakes! I was dreaming . . . the clock woke me up!

DONG DONG

Exactly eight o'clock! Twelve minutes more . . . At least . . . Now I come to think of it, my clock loses . . .

Quick, let's dial TIM and check the time . . .

. . . seconds . . . pip . . . pip . . . pip . . . At the third stroke it will be eight twelve and twenty seconds . . . Pip . . . pip . . . pip . . . At the third stroke it will be eight twelve and thirty seconds . . . pip . . . pip . . .

Help!

This is it! The end of the world!!

We're dead! . . .

No! . . . On second thoughts, we aren't dead . . . and it isn't the end of the world . . . It's nothing but an earthquake!

Oh? . . . Is THAT all it is?

I wonder how they'll explain this one at the Observatory! . . . Hello? . . . Hello? . . . Hello? . . . The telephone's not working. . . . Come on Snowy, we're going along there.

Hooray! . . . Hooray! It's only an earthquake! . . .

RRRING RRRRRING RRING

OBSERVATOR

RRRING RRRRRING RRING RRING RRRRRING

All right! All right! I'm coming!

Hooray! Hooray! . . . The end of the world has been postponed!

Hooray! Hooray! . . . It's good to be alive!

NO ENTRY

RAT TAT

NO ENTRY

NO ENTRY

Bungler! . . . Dunderhead!

What has he done?

The idiot! He made a mistake in his calculations! The meteor passed 48,000 km away from the earth, instead of colliding with it and causing the magnificent cataclysm I'd hoped for.

Never mind, Professor; you've still got it in store . . . But tell me: what about the earthquake?

Professor! . . . Professor! . . .

It has just been developed, sir. It is indeed remarkable, don't you agree, sir?

Excellent! . . . Excellent! . . . But, look there. How very extraordinary!

That group of lines, in the centre? Uranium, I presume.

Uranium? Not on your life! . . .

By the rings of Saturn! It's prodigious!

Tralala ♪ ♪ - la ♪

It may be prodigious, but it's all Greek to me!

It's prodigious! . . . Incredible! . . . Fantastic! . . . Stupefying!

My friends, I have made a sensational discovery! I have just detected a new metal! . . . A metal hitherto entirely unknown!

You've heard of the spectroscope. It's the instrument that enables us to discover elements in stars, elements not yet isolated here on the earth. This is a spectroscopic photograph of the meteor which brushed past us today. Each of these lines, or each group of lines is characteristic of a metal. Those lines in the centre represent an unknown metal, which exists in the meteor. You follow me?

Er . . . more or less . . .

I, Decimus Phostle, have discovered a new metal! I shall give my name to it: phostlite.

My heartiest congratulations!

But Professor, to get back to the meteor . . . It didn't collide with the earth, so why was there an earthquake?

Tell me, young man, do you like bull's-eyes?

Answer me. Do you or do you not like bull's-eyes?

I... er... Bull's-eyes?... I... Yes, thank you... but...

Go out and buy ten pennyworth of bull's eyes! We must have a fitting celebration of my discovery!

You were asking about the earthquake?... Oh, yes... It was caused by part of the meteor crashing to earth. As soon as we know where it fell, there we shall find phostlite!

Professor!... Professor! Listen to this...

"The polar station on Cape Morris (on the northern coast of Greenland) reports that a meteorite has undoubtedly fallen in the Arctic Ocean. Seal-hunters saw a ball of fire cross the sky and disappear over the horizon. A few seconds later the earth shook violently and icebergs cracked..."

By the rings of Saturn!

It has fallen into the sea!... It has been engulfed by the waves! And with it, my discovery! Proof of the existence of phostlite.

So that's that, Snowy. The phostlite's sunk.

This is the end! My meteorite! My phostlite!

Come on, Snowy, we'll leave him.

Poor Professor Phostle. He's terribly upset because his meteorite's fallen into the sea.

He's even forgotten to give us a bull's-eye.

OBSERVATORY

Now, what's up? Floods, this time? Or is it just a water main cracked by the earthquake?

These bricks will make stepping stones to keep my feet dry.

SPLASH

Great snakes! Why on earth didn't we think of it before?

?

You see this brick, Snowy?

Of course I can see it!...

Watch!...

Well? What d'you say?

I think that's a pretty silly joke!

Look at it Snowy . . . sticking out of the water

I can see: it's sticking out. So what?

That brick is the meteorite. The water is the Arctic Ocean. Now d'you see what I mean, Snowy?

He's as mad as a hatter!

Well? . . . What is it this time?

RRRING RRRING RRRING

NO ENTRY

RAT TAT

Professor! Professor!

I've suddenly had an idea, Professor.

An idea?

The meteorite that came down would be enormous, wouldn't it?

Of course! The violence of the earthquake proved that.

Then there's still hope. Part of such a huge mass would surely stick out of the water? . . .

By the rings of Saturn, you're right!

We must make a search and find the meteorite. We must organise an expedition. I'm sure we shall be able to obtain the capital we need from the European Foundation for Scientific Research.

We must get down to organising the expedition at once. Will you help me?

I'd be glad to.

Some time later . . .

A scientific expedition including leading European experts is leaving shortly on a voyage of discovery in Arctic waters. Its objective is to find the meteorite which recently fell in the Arctic region. It is believed that a part of the meteorite may be protruding above the surface of the water and the ice . . .

The expedition will be led by Professor Phostle, who has revealed the presence of an unknown metal in the meteorite. The other members of the party are:

. . . the Swedish scholar Eric Björgenskjöld, author of distinguished papers on solar prominences;

. . . Señor Porfirio Bolero y Calamares, of the University of Salamanca;

. . . Herr Doktor Otto Schulze, of the University of Munich;

. . . Professor Paul Cantonneau, of the University of Paris;

. . . Senhor Pedro Joàs Dos Santos, a renowned physicist, of the University of Coimbra;

. . . Tintin, the young reporter, who will represent the press;

. . . and lastly, Captain Haddock, President of the S.S.S. (Society of Sober Sailors) who will command the "Aurora", the vessel in which the expedition will embark.

Three days later . . .

Well, Snowy, the "Aurora" sails tomorrow.

We'll go aboard for our last night before setting off for Arctic waters.

I don't think much of this expedition; it'll be jolly cold up there.

AURORA

Hello . . . someone's running down the gangplank . . . That's funny . . . Stop! Who are you?

Hey there! . . . Stop!

Stop! . . .

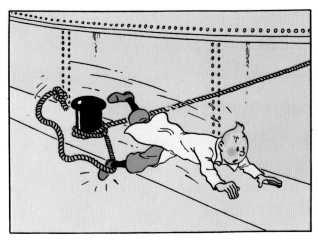

Confound that rope! . . . He's vanished . . . Now, I wonder what that fellow was doing aboard ship.

Are you on watch?

Yes.

You haven't seen anyone prowling around the deck?

No.

Oh! . . . Good! . . . Er . . . Is Captain Haddock in his cabin?

Yes.

Yes . . . No . . . Not very communicative!

Hello, where's Snowy got to? . . . Snowy . . . Snowy! SNOWY!

RAT TAT TAT TAT

Come in.

Hello, Captain. I've just seen a man bolting off the ship. He made off when I challenged him! . . . .

?

Wooah! . . . Wooah! . . . Wooah! . . .

Ah, there you are Snowy! Hey, what are you doing?

I'd say he wants us to follow him . . .

Wooah! Wooah!

Dynamite! . . . Lucky for us someone put out the fuse!

Good old Snowy! . . . He . . . well, he did his best, Captain . . .

Someone wanted to blow up the ship, or at least damage it badly. But why? . . .

One thing, if I ever lay hands on that Pyromaniac, he'll see a good display of fireworks!

Anyway, we must be on our guard. I suggest you go the rounds.

A good idea . . .

Yes, we must keep our eyes open.

You gangster, you! . . . You won't escape me!

I've got you, you rat!

Help! Help!

DYNAMITER!

SHIPWRECKER!

Come on out, centipede! Let's see you in the daylight!

Good gracious! It's Professor Phostle!

I shall complain! I shall complain to the Captain!

Professor Phostle, allow me to introduce Captain Haddock . . . You must excuse him, but we've just discovered an attempt at sabotage . . .

An attempt at sabotage? Can that be possible?

Yes, a stick of dynamite on the deck!

Fortunately Snowy had the sense to put out the fuse. But come and see . . .

?

What is it?

The dynamite! It's gone! . . .

Thundering typhoons!

?

It was there only two minutes ago! . . . I simply can't understand it.

Extraordinary!

DING DING DING

DING DING DING DING

Hey! The ship's bell!

Did you pick something up from the deck there? . . .

No . . .

Nobody here!

Ahoy there! Captain . . .

Someone's calling.

!

I am Professor Cantonneau. I would like to speak to the Captain.

That's me. I'll come down.

BANG

?

Professor Cantonneau! What has happened to him?

I've no idea. Perhaps he tripped over. His suitcase is smashed to bits . . .

He's alive!

But . . . that's my suitcase! . . . MY suitcase. I left it in your cabin.

Tell us, Professor; what happened?

I . . . I . . . don't know . . . A . . . frightful blow . . . like some huge weight falling on my head .

HA! HA! HA! HA! HA!

Ha! ha! ha! ha!

It is the judgement come upon you! Philippulus the prophet gave you warning!

He did it! . . . He dropped the suitcase!

And here is a pretty rocket I found. Now we'll have a beautiful fireworks display! . . .

The dynamite! The crazy fool! He's taken the dynamite! . . . We'll all blow up!

There's not a moment to lose!

There! . . . In half a minute this will go "whoosh"! . . .

You! I recognise you! You're the servant of Satan! Keep your distance, fiend!

!

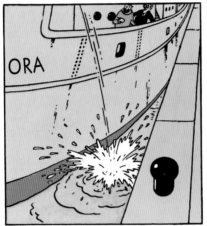

Whew! That was a close shave! I thought it would explode before it hit the water! . . .

Great snakes! What's he doing? . . . In heaven's name come down!

You speak not in the name of heaven . . . but of hell! You will never cast me down!

Higher and higher! That is my watchword!

Poor old man! He'll kill himself!

Look here, Mr Prophet, do be sensible. Come on down. Look, I'm going down, too . . .

Yes! Go down! Return to the shades of hell, whence you should never have strayed!

Please, my dear Philippulus! It is I, Phostle, Director of the Observatory. Don't you remember? . . . We worked together. Come down, I beg of you!

You are not Phostle! You have assumed his shape, but you are a fiend! . . . You are not Phostle!

But I'm Captain Haddock, by thunder . . . in command of this ship! And I order you to come down, blistering barnacles, and double quick!

I'm sorry. I take no orders, except from above! I'm staying here!

Come down, by thunder, or I'll have you clapped in irons!

Don't argue any more. I know how to bring him down.

?

You'll see. He'll come down at once . . .

Hello, hello, Philippulus the prophet! This is your guardian angel, speaking from heaven. I order you to return to earth. And be careful: don't break your neck!

Yes, sir. At once, sir. Don't be angry, sir . . .

There he is!

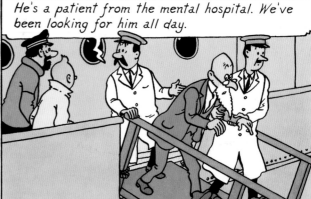

He's a patient from the mental hospital. We've been looking for him all day.

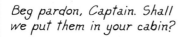

Next morning . . .

There's quite a crowd to see the "Aurora" sail.

WHARF 9

And so, listeners, the moment of departure approaches. In a few minutes the "Aurora" will sail away, heading northwards, bound for Arctic waters. A little farewell ceremony is now taking place. The committee of the Society of Sober Sailors have just presented a truly magnificent bouquet of flowers to Captain Haddock their Honorary President . . .

Goodbye, Captain, most worthy President. Never forget, the eyes of the whole world and the S.S.S. will be upon you. Good luck!

Beg pardon, Captain. Shall we put them in your cabin?

Put what, my lad?

Those . . .

WHISKY

WHISKY

WHISK

WHISK

... and here's the President of the European Foundation for Scientific Research with the leader of the expedition, Professor Phostle, handing over the flag to be planted on the meteorite.

... I entrust this flag to you, Professor, confident that it will soon fly from the summit of the meteorite. I am sure you will find it, and also the new metal, whose existence you have already announced.

Captain! Captain! ...

There's something funny going on ...

Thundering typhoons!

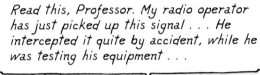
Read this, Professor. My radio operator has just picked up this signal ... He intercepted it quite by accident, while he was testing his equipment ...

São Rico. The polar ship "Peary" sailed from São Rico yesterday evening on a voyage of exploration in Arctic waters. The "Peary" will try to find the meteorite which fell in that area and which, according to experts, contains an unknown metal ...

They've stolen a march on us! They'll take possession of the meteorite! All is lost ...

Hold on, they haven't found it yet!

Tintin's right. We've still got a chance ...

ALL HANDS ABOARD SHIP! ... We sail at once!

Stand by to cast off!

TOOOOOT

(21)

The last moorings have been cast off. This is the moment of departure . . . The ship is moving slowly away from the quay. The "Aurora" has sailed . . . Sailed away in search of a shooting star . . .

You have been listening to an eyewitness account of the departure of the polar research ship "Aurora". The programme was relayed through all European networks.

Ha! ha! ha! I wish them the best of luck!

You're quite sure that they won't succeed? . . .

My dear fellow, you've been my secretary long enough to know that if the Bohlwinkel Bank has financed the "Peary" expedition, there is no question of failure. Believe me: the "Aurora" hasn't a chance.

I hope so, Mr Bohlwinkel. But still . . .

Yes I know the "Aurora" sailed sooner than I anticipated . . . The fault of that fool Hayward, bungling his job. But don't worry, I've taken care of everything . . .

Ah, good good . . .

You see, my dear fellow, the scientific expedition is just a cover for my plan to take possession of this meteorite . . . and the unknown metal Professor Phostle was naive enough to tell us about. There's a colossal fortune waiting there for us. A colossal fortune, and I don't intend to lose it!

We're on our way, Snowy . . .

This will blow away the cobwebs, eh, Snowy? What wonderful air . . . the real tang of the sea!

Yes, you can smell the fish . . .

Do as I do, Snowy. Breathe deeply. Fill your lungs with fresh air.

Let's go aft to the stern, Snowy. Anyway, it'll soon be time for lunch . . .

AURORA

Look, Snowy, there's our seaplane up there, on its catapult. It will help in our search for the meteorite.

?

Ahoy there, steward! . . . You can announce lunch. Everything's ready.

First service for luncheon!

Where's Snowy got to? I don't see him about.

Hey, steward, what's the meaning of this? The menu says "Sausages and Mash"! Right: where are the sausages?

They'll find their sea-legs in a day or two . . .

That night . . .

Impossible to sleep a wink . . . She's rolling worse than ever . . . fairly dancing a jig!

Meanwhile, in São Rico . . .

Any further news of the "Kentucky Star"?

Nothing more, Mr Bohlwinkel . . .

I've a good mind to go and join the Captain on the bridge.

Come on, Snowy we'll go to the bridge.

Great snakes! . . . It's blowing a real gale!

 Careful, Snowy, mind how you go!

 Whew! . . . I . . . honestly, I thought I'd been swept overboard. But Snowy? . . . Where's Snowy?

 Snowy!

 Snowy!! . . .

 That was a near thing, Snowy! . . . Heavens, what a storm! What a frightful storm!

 Oh, it's you . . . Nice little breeze, isn't it?

 What? . . . A breeze? Isn't this a gale?

A gale? What an idea! . . . A mere draught, that's all.

 So we aren't in any danger, then? . . .

None. Still, you've got to be careful: visibility's almost down to zero . . . and the shipping lane we're in now, the North Channel, is a pretty busy one.

 . . . Lots of ships use it . . . However, the chances of a collision are very slight . . . Each vessel has navigation lights, so . . .

 Help!

Thundering typhoons!

Hard a starboard! . . .

AURORA

Pirates! . . . Shipwreckers! . . . Sea-lice! . . . Filibusters! . . . Hoodlums! . . . Road-hogs! . . . Freshwater swabs!

Saved!

The lunatic! A little bit closer and he'd have cut us in two . . . He must be crazy sailing like that, without any lights . . . He couldn't have judged it better if he'd meant to sink us.

And why not? That might be precisely what he intended.

What do you mean?

I mean, Captain, that someone's already tried to sabotage the "Aurora" . . . the night before we sailed. The accident we just avoided looks remarkably like another attempt . . .

Thundering typhoons! . . . You're right! . . . But who on earth . . . ?

Who would be anxious to prevent us carrying out our search? Who but the "Peary" expedition, or whoever has financed it? . . .

Is that the "Kentucky Star" this time?

Yes, coming in now Mr Bohlwinkel. A radio signal . . .

S.S. Kentucky Star. Obeying orders received, attempted to sink Aurora. Operation miscarried. Awaiting instructions.

They've failed! The bungling fools! Now we're back where we started! . . . But I'll get them yet!

Oh, misery! I feel so ill! I feel horribly ill!

I feel sick . . . Ooooooh . . .

Would you mind if I opened the window a little bit? Some fresh air would do us good.

Do as you please . . . just let me die in peace.

Aaaah! . . . I feel better already.

Some days later . . .

Brrr! It's cold this morning. It feels as if we're approaching the Arctic region.

Have you noticed? It froze last night.

You ought to put on warm clothes: you'll catch cold going about like that.

You're quite right.

Come along, Snowy. We need our coats on.

I should have told him to be careful on the deck. This sheet-ice is really . . .

. . . dangerous!

Now we'll go and say good morning to the Captain.

I'm going to cause a sensation!

Here, send this by radio.

Aye, aye, captain.

M.S. Aurora to President, E.F.S.R. In sight of Iceland. Putting into port at Akureyri, in Eyjafjördur, for refuelling. All well on board.

Here, Mr Bohlwinkel: it's a message sent by the "Aurora" to the European Foundation for Scientific Research. Our wireless operator just intercepted it.

Give it me.

Aha! . . . They're putting in at an Icelandic port! Excellent! Excellent! I think, my dear Johnson, that their stay will be a long one . . . Let us begin by sending a short note. Take this down, Johnson . . .

I'm ready, sir . . .

Bohlwinkel Bank to Smithers, general agent for Golden Oil, Reykjavik, Iceland. Circulate following order immediately to all agents for Golden Oil in Iceland: Absolute prohibition against refuelling polar vessel Aurora . . . There! Have that sent in the secret code.

Right, Mr Bohlwinkel.

The next morning . . .

So here we are in Akureyri. Shall we be staying here long, Captain?

Oh, no . . .

Just long enough to fill up with oil. Then we set out for Greenland.

There. I'm going to order the fuel. It won't take a minute.

Right. I'll wait for you here.

Good morning. I want my ship refuelled with oil.

Very good. What's the name of your vessel?

Polar research ship "Aurora". Captain Haddock.

Oh? . . . You're the Captain of . . . of the "Aurora"?

Oh! . . . I . . . I've bad news for you, Captain. I suddenly remembered, we haven't a drop of fuel oil in stock . . .

What's that you say? No fuel oil? . . . That's absurd! I've got to have oil, d'you hear?

I assure you that I can't . . . I mean, I haven't got any oil!

That sounds like an argument . . .

It's disgraceful, I tell you! Disgraceful!

Remember! On your own head be it!

AGENCY GOLDEN OIL

Well? . . . Well? . . . What happened?

There's no fuel to be had from Golden Oil. Not a drop!

So what? We'll ask someone else, that's all.

Someone else? Golden Oil have a monopoly of the sale of fuel oil throughout the country.

But that means . . . We're stuck here?

Yes, stuck. And in the meantime . . .

. . . the "Peary" continues her voyage!

Can't you look what you're doing, you seismic semaphore?

Me? A semaphore? . . . You, why you're nothing but a . . .

Oh!

Fidgy! . . . Fidgy! . . . Fidgy! . . .

Fidgy! . . . Fidgy! . . . Fidgy! . . .

Boodle, boodle, boodle!

Boodle, boodle, boodle! . . .

Aye, aye, ayeyeee!

Aye, aye, ayeyeee!

?

Dear old Chester! . . . Just the same as ever!

My dear Captain Haddock! You haven't changed a bit!

Tintin, let me introduce you to an old friend: Captain Chester, a shipmate of mine for more than twenty years.

I'm glad to hear it. I thought you were going to kill each other!

You're waiting to refuel?

You've said it! . . . What a country! . . . Not a drop of oil in the whole of this one-horse island!

No fuel? . . . But they've got plenty at Golden Oil. I was there just now. They're filling up my trawler "Sirius" tomorrow morning.

What? Someone's been having me on!

Ten thousand thundering typhoons! I'll teach those pirates to play fast and loose with Captain Haddock!

Gang of thieves! . . . Black marketeers! . . . Monopolizers! . . . Turncoats! . . . Ophicleides! . . . Colocynths!

Haddock!

Don't stop me! I'm going to exterminate those crooks! . . . The twisters!

Haddock, listen to me.

Calm down, Captain!

Listen to me. You're wasting your time. Do you know who's financed the "Peary" expedition? No? It was announced on the radio this morning. The Bohlwinkel Bank of São Rico.

So what? I don't mind! Blistering barnacles. I need fuel oil! . . .

All right, all right. D'you know who owns Golden Oil? . . . No? . . . The Bohlwinkel Bank, of São Rico. Now d'you understand?

?

Let me go! . . . I'm going to tear those caterpillars into little pieces!

Wait, Captain, I've got an idea!

An idea? About getting fuel oil?

Yes.

Come on, we'll discuss this over a glass of whisky. Let's go into this bar.

Barman! A bottle of whisky, and three glasses.

No whisky for me, thanks.

I'll have tonic water . . .

Two glasses, barman. And some tonic water for the lad.

By Jupiter, I've just remembered . . . I forgot you're the President of the Society of Sober Sailors. You don't drink whisky, of course. Tonic for you as well?

You're right . . . Tonic water . . . Good idea . . .

That's enough! . . . Thanks.

Here's to you, Haddock!

And to you! . . . Look, just to please you, I'll take a drop of whisky with my tonic . . . For old time's sake . . .

Only a drop . . . A thimbleful . . .

That's enough . . . Thanks!

Aaaaaaaaah! . . . The tonic in these parts does you a power of good!

Now, tell us your idea.

Look, where is your ship moored?

Yes, where's she moored, the "Sisi" . . . the "Sirius"?

Just astern of the "Aurora".

That's fine! . . . And you're refuelling tomorrow morning? . . . Splendid! . . . Now, listen . . .

Li-li-listen carefully, Chester. This boy always has ex-x-x-x-cellent ideas.

The next morning . . .

GOLDEN OIL II

I say, Captain, d'you think there's a leak in your tanks? They don't seem to be filling.

OK, OK . . . They're big ones, that's all. Keep on pumping.

SIRIUS

ORA

That's the lot, Captain! Our tanks are full . . .

Will you send off this cable?

"Smithers, Golden Oil, Reykjavik. Your orders carried out. Aurora stays here until new instructions received. Signed: Payne." That'll be seven   krónur.

TOOOOOT

TELEGRAPH

Good. That's the "Sirius" going out . . .

It's not the "Sirius"! . . . It's the "Aurora"!!

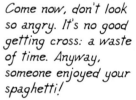

A week later . . .

This is where we are. We've crossed the 72nd parallel. You will confine your search to an area between 73 and 78 North, and 8 and 13 West . . . You understand?

Right.

Above all, don't take risks: don't go beyond the limits we fixed.

And don't forget to maintain contact by radio. Goodbye, and good luck. Keep your eyes skinned for the meteorite.

AURORA

There they go . . .

Let's hope they don't run into any trouble.

Hello? . . . Hello? . . .

Hello? . . . Receiving you loud and clear . . . What? . . . You've seen something?

The meteorite?

Something peculiar. The sky's quite clear. But there's a great column of white vapour rising from one spot about 20° East.

33

How extraordinary. They've seen a great column of white vapour on the horizon.

Quick! . . . Give me the microphone.

This is Professor Phostle. Tell me, does the column of vapour seem to be coming from a definite point? . . . You say there are no other clouds in sight? The sky is clear?

That's it! . . . They've found the meteorite!!

Careful! . . . The earphones . . .

Forgive me. I forgot! Yes, Captain, it's the meteorite causing the column of vapour. The heat emitted from it has already melted the ice. Gradually the water surrounding it is warming up.

Thus water-vapour is created, and this is rising up to form the clouds which they have seen.

Blistering barnacles!

Hello? Hello? . . . You have found the meteorite! . . . Hooray! . . . Hello? . . . Are you receiving me?

Hello? . . . Hello? . . . Hello? . . . They're not answering any more! . . .

Tell me, Captain, should these wires be connected to anything? . . .

Thundering typhoons! . . . The leads weren't plugged in!

There! That's fixed it.

Hello? . . . Ah, you can hear me . . . Turn round and come back . . . The vapour is caused by the meteorite . . . yes . . . Come back, you've completed your mission.

All right, we're returning.

Look down there! . . .

Hello? . . . Yes? . . . What did you say? Smoke? . . . Smoke from a ship? . . . Where? . . . In which direction?

Bearing west-south-west. Yes, we're heading in that direction . . .

Hello? . . . Yes . . . They're steering towards the column of vapour? Thundering typhoons! . . . It's the "Peary", isn't it? . . .

It's not possible to identify her yet . . . But we'll soon know . . .

Well? What's the ship called? . . . Did you see?

The "Peary"!

They're heading for the meteorite . . . We're coming back - fast!

Meanwhile . . .

R.S. Peary, 12°23' W., 76°40' N., to Bohlwinkel, São Rico. Have been spotted by E.F.S.R. aircraft. Presume Aurora in vicinity. We are putting on steam.

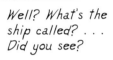

I'm worried. I keep wondering how they'll manage to land without hitting one of those confounded icebergs . . .

There they are!

They're preparing to land . . . It'll be a miracle if they don't smash themselves up on an iceberg!

Well, Snowy old boy, if we get out of this in one piece we'll be lucky!

Thundering typhoons! . . . They scraped against that one . . . and that one too! . . . Whew! They just missed it!

We're done for this time, Snowy!

E.F.S.R.

Hooray! He's a real ace!

E.F.S.R.

What news?

We haven't a moment to lose, Captain . . .

S.R.

The "Peary" is two hundred and fifty km ahead of us. We must overtake her!

Two hundred and fifty km ahead!!

This is the end . . . We've lost the race.

E.F.S.R.

No, Captain, we're not finished yet. Come on, let's have a look at the chart.

It's useless.

Look, the "Peary" is there . . . And this is our position. Our maximum speed is **16** knots. The "Peary" can't do more than **12** knots. We could therefore gain on them by **6** km each hour. They're **250** km ahead. So in **37½** hours we'd have caught up with the "Peary" . . .

Yes, unless they'd reached the meteorite by then . . .

Captain, we must try to overtake the "Peary"! . . . This is no moment to throw up the sponge, just when victory is in sight.

Tintin's right; we must try, Captain.

That's all very fine! . . . But to catch up 250 km! . . .

Impossible! . . . It's quite futile to try. We're going to turn round and go home . . .

All right . . . er . . . I say, Captain, I'm frozen to death after that reconnaissance flight. I think I need a little whisky . . .

Some whisky? You? . . . er . . . I'll just see if there is any . . .

You'll have a glass with us, won't you, Captain?

You bet I will!

On second thoughts. I really do think the game is up. It'd be far better to give up the struggle . . .

!

Give up the struggle? . . . Never! . . . Blistering barnacles, this is no moment to throw up the sponge, just when victory is in sight! Thundering typhoons! . . . We'll show those P-P-Patagonian p-p-pirates what we can do! . . . The l-l-lily-livered l-l-landlubbers!

Come on! We shall see what we shall see! . . . Show a leg! On deck with you!

Get on with it, Chief! Thundering typhoons! jump to it! . . . Full speed ahead! The enemy have 250 km start on us: we've got to catch them up!

Cox'n at the wheel! Stick to your course. Steer North by East. And watch out for icebergs!

Aye, aye, sir.

Noon next day . . .

Hooray! . . . There she is! . . . That's smoke from the "Peary"!

We're steaming faster than she is! . . . We'll overtake them this evening, or during the night.

Captain! . . . A signal!

!

Read it! . . . This is the last straw! . . . What are we going to do? Blistering barnacles, what are we going to do?

!

Ask our scientists to come to the saloon. Tell them I have important news . . .

Gentlemen, I'd like to read you a signal we've just picked up. It's a distress call. The text is disjointed, as if the transmitter was damaged. Even the name of the ship is incomplete.

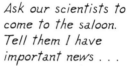

S.O.S. S.O.S. S.O.S. CIT... 70°45' N., 19°12' W. IN COLLISION WITH ICEB... TAKING WATER IN FORWA.. ..QUEST ASSISTANCE URGE...

There it is, gentlemen. Either we can go to the aid of this ship, and abandon all hope of reaching the meteorite before the "Peary", or else we can continue on our course, and not answer this call . . . It's up to you to decide.

There's no question about it, Captain. Human lives are in danger. We must go to their aid, even if it does cost us our prize . . .

I was sure of your answer, Professor. We'll go about right away . . .

Bravo!

Come on. We must reply, and let them know we're coming to their assistance . . .

I've forgotten to shut that confounded door again . . .

Polar research ship Aurora to Cit . . . in distress. Your message received. We are steaming towards you. Keep in touch with us. Good luck!

Well?

That's the third time I've sent out the message . . . There's no reply.

I suppose their radio has packed up for good . . .

Yes, unless . . .

Unless they have . . . gone down? Is that what you mean to say?

No, it's not that . . .

Captain, will you let me send out a message myself?

Naturally, but . . .

Is that the text of what you want to send? It's absurd! What does the ship's name matter to us? . . . Anyway, you'll spend all night waiting for replies.

All night. Yes, I know.

You do as you like, but I think it's absolutely crazy. I'm going to turn in. Good night!

Good night, Captain . . . There. Could you send that off?

Right.

Polar research ship Aurora to all shipping companies. Please will all companies owning ships with name commencing "CIT" please advise us immediately of full names of these ships. Also inform us if one is in distress, position 70°45' N., 19°12' W.

The next morning . . .

Good morning, boys! How goes it? Anyone answered your message?

Is that all? . . . Well, what is the name of the ship in distress?

I still don't know! Here, look for yourself.

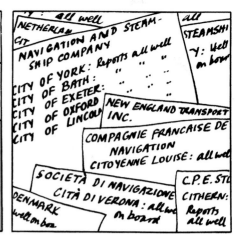

NETHERLAN NAVIGATION AND STEAMSHIP COMPANY
CITY OF YORK: Reports all well
CITY OF BATH: " " . .
CITY OF EXETER: " " . .
CITY OF OXFORD NEW ENGLAND TRANSPORT INC.
CITY OF LINCOL
COMPAGNIE FRANCAISE DE NAVIGATION
CITOYENNE LOUISE: all well
SOCIETA DI NAVIGAZIONE CITTÀ DI VERONA : all we on board
DENMARK well on boa
C.P.E. ST
CITHERN: Reports all well
all well
STEAMSHI
Y: Well on boar

A fat lot of progress you've made! You don't even know the name . . .

Ssh! . . . There's another signal coming through.

Well?

We've got it. Here at last, the name of the ship. She's the "Cithara".

John Kingsby Navigation Company to Polar research ship Aurora. S.S. Cithara in distress 70°45' N., 19°12' W.

Now you've got what you want! There's your answer. She's the "Cithara" owned by the John Kingsby Company.

What are you looking for now? Her tonnage? Or her Captain's age? . . . Tell me, what more do you want to know?

Just one last detail, Captain. I think it will interest you. The "Cithara" does NOT exist!

!?

What do you mean? . . . Look here, that's impossible!

It's true, Captain! . . . The "Cithara" does not exist. Nor does the John Kingsby Navigation Company. The names don't appear in the register of shipping! Someone has sent us a fake S.O.S.!

A fake S.O.S.! . . . A fake S.O.S.! . . . Could the "Peary" have sent out the call to delay us? . . . No! No sailor would ever do that.

A sailor? No. But what about the expedition's sponsors? . . .

Billions of blue blistering barnacles! Pirates! They'll need a distress signal when I get hold of them!

Here. Send out the following message: Polar research Ship Aurora to bogus John Kingsby Company . . . er . . . Deeply shocked by subterfuge . . . no . . . that's not strong enough . . . er . . . Gangsters! . . . that's it . . . Gangsters! Twisters! Traitors! . . . Woodlice! . . . Turncoats! . . . Ship-wreckers! . . . Mountebanks! Moujiks! Signed: Haddock.

Quick, Captain, we must take up the chase!

And add: Rhizopods and Ectoplasms!

Helmsman ahoy! Wheel hard a starboard!

Hello, engine-room! . . . We're going after the "Peary" again. Increase your speed!

I wonder if we can possibly catch up with them . . .

Increase speed, Captain? . . . It's impossible . . . We're going all out already!

I don't care how you do it! . . . But we must go faster!

A fake S.O.S. . . . The pirates! . . . You know, if it hadn't been for you, we'd still be going south! . . . By the way, what first aroused your suspicions?

Thundering typhoons! What's the matter?

I think I must have fallen asleep . . .

It's true, you've been up all night. Go and get some sleep now.

You're right. I'll go to my cabin for an hour or so.

Have a good rest.

Snowy! . . . Come on, Snowy.

Whoever invented a ladder like this? You can see he never owned a dog!

Snowy? . . . Are you coming?

I'm too fagged out to undress. I'm asleep on my feet . . .

Still, you might remove my best bib and tucker.

Well, Snowy old boy, here's one who's going to sleep like a log.

RAT TAT TAT

Yes?

It's me! Open up, quick! . . .

All right, coming . . .

Read this: it's a signal we've intercepted, from the "Peary".

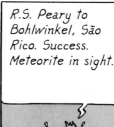

R.S. Peary to Bohlwinkel, São Rico. Success. Meteorite in sight.

They've beaten us! . . . We're finished!

WOOAH!

No, we're not finished yet . . . The seaplane, Captain! Have the seaplane made ready . . .

. . . and warn the pilot. We're leaving right away.

OK

Hey! What about our sleep?

Now, Snowy, you've got to stay here till I come back . . .

Don't be silly, Snowy; I'll soon be back.

Oh Columbus! . . . They haven't seen him! Poor Snowy!

Oh my goodness!

The radio! . . . We must warn them by radio! . . .

Hello? . . . Hello? . . . Hello? . . . Snowy's gone with you! . . . Yes, Snowy . . . He's clinging to the port wing of your aircraft.

We must land.

No, we've no time to lose . . .

Hello? . . . Hello? . . . Snowy is safe! Yes, I've got him here with me . . .

We're getting near . . . There's the cloud of vapour rising from the meteorite . . .

Some time later . . .

Hello, hello? . . . Captain Haddock here. Any news?

There isn't a single iceberg in sight, and the cloud of vapour is much nearer. We certainly can't be very far away now.

The meteorite! There's the meteorite!

Hello . . . Tintin here . . . We can see the meteorite!!

Really? You mean that? . . . You can see the meteorite! . . . Hooray! . . . What's it like?

It forms an island, sloping gently towards the west, and . . . Great snakes! . . . The "Peary" has beaten us to it!

The "Peary" has beaten them to it.

Tell me . . . I suppose their flag is already flying from the top of the meteorite?

Their flag? . . . Wait . . . No, I can't see a flag . . .

Hooray! Then there's still hope!

Perhaps. I can just make out what's happening aboard the "Peary" . . . it looks as if . . . as if . . .

Yes . . . they're just lowering a boat . . .

This is it! The meteorite is ours!

"PEARY"

RRRRRRRRR

Hello! That sounds like an engine to me . . .

There, Captain, it's an aircraft!

It's the seaplane from the "Aurora", confound it!

Bah! By the time they've come down on the sea and launched their rubber dinghy, our men will be ashore on the meteorite.

E.F.S.R

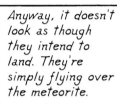

Anyway, it doesn't look as though they intend to land. They're simply flying over the meteorite.

Wooah!

E.F.S.R

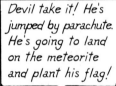

Devil take it! He's jumped by parachute. He's going to land on the meteorite and plant his flag!

Crumbs! . . . The flag! . . .

That was lucky!

There he goes! He'll arrive before us!

No! I know how to stop him!

"PEARY"

Quick! Quick!

I can't do it. The cord won't come undone . . .

Look! He's planted his flag!

E.F.S.R.

E.F.S.R.

E.F.S.R.

Victory! Our flag is flying over the meteorite!

Victory!!

E.F.S.R.

There he is, landing.

Snowy's coming to join you. He won't stay with me any longer.

Wooah!

Come on then, Snowy . . .

E.F.S.R.

?

Wooaaaaah!

E.F.S.R.

48

Snowy, my poor Snowy! . . . You must have banged against a rock!

Wooaaaaaah!

OW! OWW! . . .

Ow! . . . Yow! . . . Yeow!

Wooaah!

The water's boiling! . . .

E.F.S.R.

Hello? . . . Hello? . . . Hello? . . .

Hello, I am receiving you . . . Yes . . . What? Serious . . . three days . . . Yes, of course. Good. Right . . .

The "Aurora" has developed engine trouble and has had to reduce speed. She won't be here for three days. We can't wait: we have no supplies. So we must get back and rejoin her. Anyway, our mission is accomplished. Are you coming?

It's impossible. Someone must stay here to guard the island: that's only sense. So, what's to be done?

There's only one answer: I'll stay here and wait for you to come back with supplies. All right?

Tintin, you don't mean we're going to stay all by ourselves on this island?

Right . . . I've got my emergency rations: a few biscuits, an apple and a flask of fresh water. I'll leave them with you.

E.F.S.R.

There . . .

Thanks.

Goodbye. And good luck. I'll be back in the morning.

There he goes.

I'll be glad when he's back!

 Now, Snowy, we'll have something to eat . . .

Good idea!

 An apple, ship's biscuits and water: starvation, Snowy!

And how!

 Starvation . . . that reminds me of Philippulus the prophet, with his predictions of hunger and cold!

 And that nightmare when he was threatening me: "The judgement! . . . Yea! . . . Behold the judgement!"

 And the judgement was an enormous spider. Brrr! I still go cold at the thought of it . . .

 A spider!

 Squash it, Tintin!

 It's disappeared among the rocks.

 Leave it. Come on, Snowy . . .

 Enjoy your supper, Snowy. Let's forget that prophet of doom, with his spiders and his "dong-dong-dong".

 DONG DONG DONG !

 What an ass I am. It's the bell on the "Peary".

DONG DONG DONG

 It's their supper-time too, I expect . . .

 Finished already, Snowy? I'm afraid I've nothing else for you. The two biscuits left are for tomorrow.

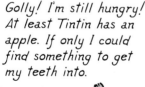 Golly! I'm still hungry! At least Tintin has an apple. If only I could find something to get my teeth into.

 Ugh, there's a maggot in this apple . . .

Not a thing . . .

 Whoops!

 Are you coming, Snowy? We're going to turn in now. I'm absolutely dead beat.

Our parachute will come in handy again. We can use it for a mattress and as a blanket.

Lucky for us the air is quite warm. It's extraordinary, when we're so near the Pole.

Good night, Snowy. Keep a good look out . . .

BOOM

?

I thought I heard an explosion . . . Hello, the "Peary" has disappeared. She must have weighed anchor while we were asleep!

Still, that explosion? . . . I suppose I was dreaming . . .

BOOM

Tintin, I'm s . . . s . . . scared!

I've got it! It must be the island itself. It's probably a kind of small volcano . . . or a volcanic vent of some sort.

No! Not a sign of a crack, nor of a crater . . . So, now what?

!
Wooah! Wooah!

Snowy's found something: he looks pleased with himself!

An egg! . . . A egg!! . . . Great snakes! . . . Who can have laid that?

Come on, Tintin, let's scramble it.

But . . . but . . . Unless I'm seeing things . . . The egg: it's getting bigger!

It's not an egg! It's a mushroom! . . .

The mushroom . . . vaporised, vanished into thin air!

BOOM

Things seem to be calming down a bit . . .

BOOM

Yes, it's over. Whew! If that's the effect of the new metal, we're in for some more surprises!

Ssh! . . .

No, nothing. The sky is empty . . .

I thought I heard a buzzing, like the noise of an engine . . .

!

An apple tree! . . . Good heavens, it's an apple tree! . . . It must have been the core I threw away yesterday . . . It's incredible! . . . Fantastic! . . .

I'm keeping an eye open in case the tree blows up too.

It must be magic!

! WOOAAAH!

Shoo!! . . . Get away, you horrible creature!

Where did that huge insect come from? It can't be . . . Yes, it must have been from the maggot I found in the apple!

Well, Snowy old man, if everything's going to start growing bigger, we're in a fine jam!

But . . . but . . . the spider! . . . The spider that escaped out of the box, last night . . .

I say, Tintin you don't think that will have grown, too?

If it's still alive it should be near the apple tree: that's where I was sitting yesterday.

Careful! . . . It might appear at any moment . . .

? THUMP

Great snakes!

THUMP

THUMP

? ?

An earthquake! That's the last straw!

And what's that rumbling?

Help! That huge wave will swamp everything!

Whew! . . . Safe! The water isn't coming up any further.

I say, the whole island has tilted right over.

In the meantime more apple trees have sprung up.

Hey, what about the spider?

Ssh! . . . Quiet! . . .

This time I'm sure of it . . . I can hear the sound of an engine.

There Snowy! . . . The seaplane . . .

Hooray! . . . We're saved!

Oh, what a beautiful ♩ ♩ ♪ mo-o-orming! ♩ ♪ ♫

Oh, what a tra-la la-la! ♪ ♫ ♩

Tra-la-la-la-la-la-la-a-a-la ♭ ♭ ♭

Everything's going my way! ♫

Crumbs! What a monster!

If only I can grab a stone . . .

Got one! . . . And it hasn't budged . . .

Now, take a good aim . . .

Missed it!

Great snakes! another earthquake!

Whew! That was close! Thank goodness for the apple tree!

Hello? Hello? . . . The meteorite has just been shaken by an earthquake. The whole thing has tilted over, and is sinking slowly into the sea.

What did you say? . . . An earthquake? . . . The meteorite is sinking? . . . What about Tintin? Where is he?

We're losing the meteorite?

Can't see him . . . Oh, yes . . . He's lying at the foot of an enormous tree, quite still. The water will soon reach him.

Try to land! . . . Tintin must be saved!

Impossible to get down, Captain. The sea's absolutely raging!

Tintin! . . . Tintin! . . . Wake up!

Not a flicker. And the water's still rising! . . . What can I do?

WOOAH! . . . WOOAH! . . .

It's no good! . . . But he simply must come round!

OWW!

What's got into you, Snowy? Why did you bite me?

Quick, we must get a move on!

Now what's happening? . . . Great snakes! The meteorite's tipping over!

Quick, up to the top. The island is settling more and more . . .

Here goes! It's neck or nothing! I simply must save him!

E.F.S.R.

What's he doing? . . . Is he going to land? . . . It's sheer lunacy!

I can't see him any more. I hope to heaven he hasn't crashed . . .

He made it! He managed to get down safely!

Now he's hidden by the waves again . . .

Hooray! He's succeeded in launching the rubber dinghy.

I can't come any closer: I'd be dashed on the rocks. I'll throw you a line with a life-jacket attached. Haul in the line and put the life-jacket on.

Right!

Here quickly, Snowy. We'll try to reach the dinghy . . .

Jump in? . . . Me? Never again!

Snowy! . . . Snowy! . . . Come on, come here at once!

I don't want to go in the water! . . . Wow! . . . Wow!

All right, stop crying. You aren't going in the water.

I'll throw you! Catch!

One . . . two . . .

No, he might fall in the sea. I'll try another way.

Come on, Snowy, get in!

?

That's Snowy safe! Now it's my turn. But first . . .

. . . I'll replace the flag. It must fly over the meteorite to the end.

E.F.S.R.

I'll throw you the rope, and you can haul me across.

Right!

Here goes!

Got you!

Safe at last!

Now, let's get out of here, fast!

What an idiot I am!

?

What are you doing? It's madness to go back!

For heaven's sake come back! You'll go down with the meteorite!

We must have a lump of the mineral . . . for Professor Phostle. Otherwise all our efforts will have been wasted!

Quick! . . . Catch!

Tintin! . . . I can't see Tintin!

No sign of Tintin . . .

Yes, there, hanging on to the lump of phostlite . . . with the flag, too!

Meanwhile . . .

Nothing . . . not a word . . . What's become of them?

It's them! . . . I've got them! . . . Hello? . . . Hello? . . .

The seaplane?

Hello? . . . Yes . . . Yes . . . Yes . . . Good!

The meteorite? What of the meteorite?

They're returning! . . . They're safe and sound! . . . Hooray!

Some hours later . . .

There they are! There they are!

Here you are, I've brought you a lump of phostlite . . . wrapped in the expedition's flag.

E.F

Look out!

BOOM

Some weeks later . . .

The polar research ship "Aurora", which sailed in search of the meteorite that fell in the Arctic, will soon be back in home waters. The expedition succeeded in finding the meteorite, just before it was submerged by the waves - probably as a result of some underwater upheaval. Happily, thanks to the courage and presence of mind shown by the young reporter Tintin, alone on the island at the very moment . . .

. . . when it was engulfed by the sea, it was possible to save a lump of the metal divined in the meteorite by Professor Phostle. Members of the expedition have already verified the remarkable properties of the metal; examination of it will undoubtedly be of extraordinary scientific interest. We may therefore look forward to more sensational disclosures.

It is now known that certain incidents that occurred during the voyage of the "Aurora" were unquestionably deliberate acts of sabotage designed to cripple the expedition. Those responsible will soon be exposed, and their leader unmasked. This master criminal is reported to be a powerful São Rico financier. He will shortly be brought to justice.

Have you noticed how preoccupied the Captain has been lately?

Yes, I'll try to find out the trouble.

What's up, Captain? . . . Is something the matter?

!

LAND HO! LAND HO!

Thundering typhoons! Land . . . and about time, too!

Why? . . . Are we out of fuel-oil?

Worse than that! . . . We're out of whisky!!

THE END
